TWO OLD POTATOES AND ME

Words by John Coy · Pictures by Carolyn Fisher

Alfred A. Knopf · New York

For my dad, who taught me how to grow potatoes, and everything else.

—J.C.

Thanks to Norton Stillman for the idea.

For Stevie. —C.F.

THIS IS A BORZOI BOOK PUBLISHED BY ALFRED A. KNOPF

Text copyright © 2003 by John Coy

Illustrations copyright © 2003 by Carolyn Fisher

All rights reserved under International and Pan-American Copyright conventions.

Published in the United States by Alfred A. Knopf, an imprint of Random House Children's Books, a division of Random House, Inc., New York, and simultaneously in Canada by Random House of Canada Limited, Toronto.

Distributed by Random House, Inc., New York.

www.randomhouse.com/kids

KNOPF, BORZOI BOOKS, and the colophon are registered trademarks of Random House, Inc.

Library of Congress Cataloging-in-Publication Data

Coy, John, 1958-

Two old potatoes and me / words by John Coy; pictures by Carolyn Fisher.

p. cm.

Summary: After a young girl finds two old potatoes at her father's house, they plant and tend them to see if they will have new potatoes in September.

ISBN 0-375-82180-5 (trade) — ISBN 0-375-92180-X (lib. bdg.)

[1. Fathers and daughters–Fiction. 2. Potatoes–Fiction. 3. Divorce–Fiction.] I. Fisher, Carolyn, ill. II. Title.

PZ7.C839455Tw 2003

[E]–dc21

2002043261

Printed in the United States of America

June 2003

10 9 8 7 6 5 4 3 2 1

First Edition

Last spring at my dad's house, I found

two old potatoes

in the back of the cupboard.

they were so OLD.

sprouts were growing

from their eyes.

"Gross."

I tossed them in the TRASH

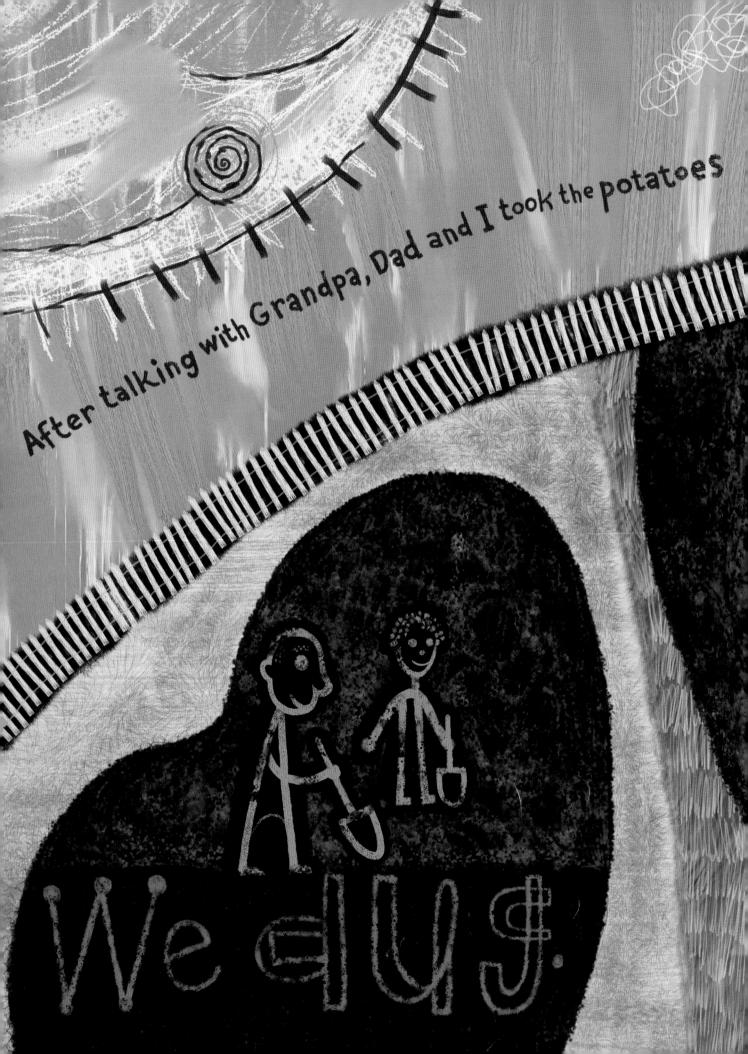

After talking with Grandpa, Dad and I took the potatoes

Dad carefully cut the potatoes into nine pieces with his jackknife.

I made sure each piece had at least one yellow sprout.

Dad dug nine small holes. I put a piece of potato, with the eye facing up, in each hole.

Then I covered them with dirt to make little hills.

Dad got the hose

and I watered gently.

In May,

green plants poked up
like caterpillars unfolding.

We got down
on our knees

and picked weeds.

We shoveled compost onto each hill.

"Won't that smother the plants?"

"No. They'll grow through it."

"Are we really going to get new potatoes from old potatoes?"

"I think so," said Dad.

IN JUNE,

the plants grew bigger, violet flowers blossomed, and we added more compost.

When we watered, I accidentally sprayed my dad with the hose.

He laughed and sprayed me back.

IN JULY, when the plants were as tall as my waist, we picked potato beetles off the leaves. I dropped them into a pail of soapy water.

GROSS!

"We have to do this," Dad said.

otherwise, the bugs will eat the leaves and the potatoes won't grow."

In August,
some of the plants
turned brown and withered.

"Are they dead?"
"No," said Dad.

"The potatoes are
growing underground."

"Are you sure?"
"I hope so.
That's what your
grandpa said."

We weeded

We Watered.

We Waited.

Now, on a cool September day,

Dad and I sit on the bench in front of the garden.

"How's your bedroom at your mom's house coming?" Dad asks.

"Good. Mom and I painted it periwinkle."

"Periwinkle. I like that color. I bet it looks good."

"You can see it on Friday when you pick me up."

"Okay," Dad says. "It will be Periwinkle Friday."

We get up
and walk to the garden.
"What's your favorite way
to eat potatoes?" Dad asks.

"MASHED,
with lots of butter and
a sprinkle of nutmeg for good luck."

Dad gets the garden fork from the shed and I carry the big bucket.

Dad digs at the first hill. Nothing but dirt. He digs again. More dirt.

I dig deep. I lift the fork and see seven golden shapes. "Potatoes!" I shout.

"Look at those SPUDS," Dad says.

I bend down,
pick up a potato,
rub the dirt off its skin,
and set it in the bucket.

ONE potato,

two potato,

THREE Potato,

four

Five SIX
potato,
PoTATo
SEVEN
PoTATO,

MorE

51 Potato, 52 Potato, 53 Potato, 54
55 Potato, 56 Potato, 57 Potato

more

Mashed Potatoes

2 pounds of potatoes (Yukon Golds are a favorite)
1/2 teaspoon of salt
1/2 stick (4 tablespoons) of butter
1/2 cup of milk (heated)
A sprinkle of nutmeg

Peel the potatoes and cut them into equal-sized cubes.
Put the potatoes in a pan, cover with cold water,
and add the salt.
Bring the water to a boil, reduce the heat,
and simmer until the potatoes are tender.
Drain the potatoes in a colander.
Return the potatoes to pan
and heat for one minute to dry.
Turn off the heat and stir the potatoes
with a wooden spoon.
Mash with a masher.
Add the butter.
Mash some more.
Add the hot milk.
Stir until smooth with the wooden spoon.
Add a sprinkle of nutmeg for good luck.

Enjoy!